v	W
ng	V
w	Oo
z	Ng
oo	Z

ten rabbits hop,
1
2
3
4
5
6
7
8
9
10

a hundred bees buzz,

twelve rooks flock,

and seven elves sit on toadstools.

A snoozing elf has a rest.
Zzzzzz

A vain elf looks at himself.

A singing elf hums a jazz song.

A strong elf lifts up twigs,

and an elf in a green smock paints...

...twin elves in red velvet coats.

seven elves
1
2
3
4
5
6
7